SHAPED BY TEARS

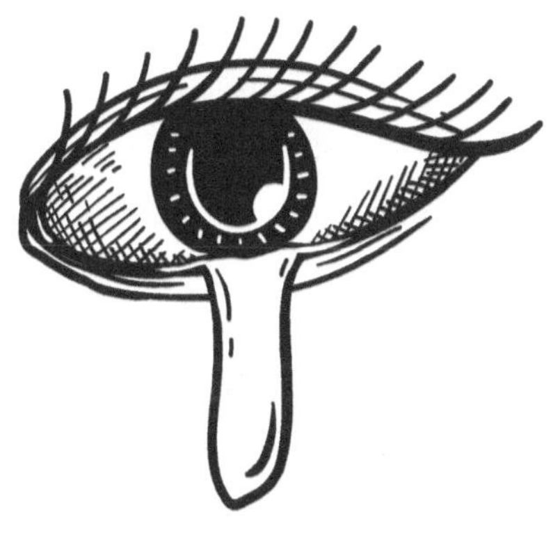

Taylor Quill

Copyright Page
© 2024 by Taylor Quill

TABLE OF CONTENTS

01 The Roots of Pain

07 The Weight of Tears

13 Breaking the Chains

19 Pruning the Heart

25 The Storm Within

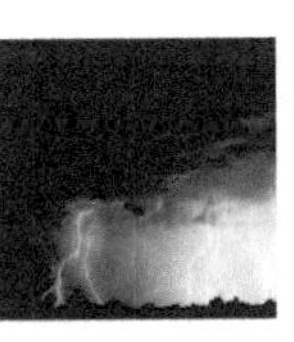

31 Finding Faith in the Fall

37 Repositioning the Soul

43 The Lessons in Every Tear

49 Blossoming Through Adversity

55 Peace in the Purpose

62 Final Note

63 About the Author

$\rightarrow$

CHAPTER ONE

The Roots of Pain

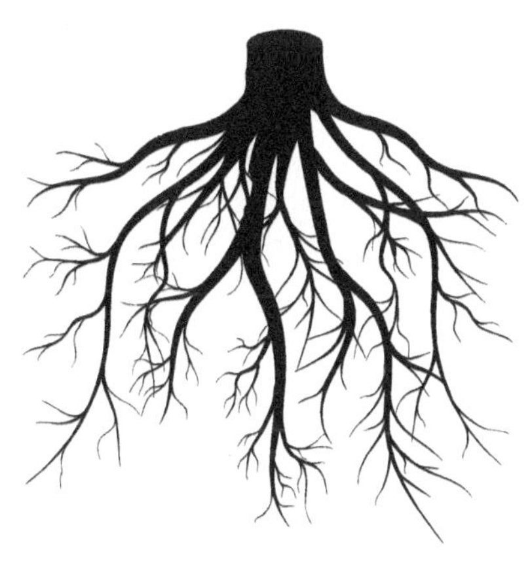

The First Step

In the soil of silence, a seed was sown,
Planted in darkness, yet deep it had grown.
Roots twisted tightly, tangled and frail,
Fed by the echoes of every harsh wail.

I taste the bitterness in each breath I take,
A poison so sweet, I can't seem to break.
I feel it inside, the thorns in my chest,
The weight of the past that won't let me rest.

Silent as shadows, my sorrow does creep,
In the cracks of my heart, where it silently
weeps.

But from this dark soil, will light ever grow?
Or will the roots deepen, and endless pain
flow?

Beneath the Surface

Beneath my skin, the storm rages on,
Thunderous whispers of where I went wrong.
I taste the ashes of dreams turned to dust,
Feel the sting of betrayal, the crumbling trust.

Trembling hands grip the past I can't see,
But it echoes in shadows, still haunting me.
I hear the silent screams of long-locked fears,
And smell the fragrance of unspoken tears.

The roots of my pain, buried deep in my veins,
They grow with each loss, they thrive in my chains.

I feel them twisting, pulling me down—
As the weight of my past keeps me bound.

Broken Ground

Cracks in the earth where my soul once stood,
Shattered like glass in the warmth of the flood.
I hear the cries of my heart, breaking apart,
A melody fractured, the sound of the start.

The taste of the earth, so bitter and cold,
My fingers dig deeper, seeking what's bold.
I feel every shard of a broken embrace,
The touch of despair that time cannot erase.

In the roots of my pain, there's a truth I must face:I've built my own chains, and I've kept my own pace.

But the soil is rich, and the wounds are wide—
From these roots, perhaps I can rise.

The Burden of Roots

The roots of my pain are heavy and old,
Gnarled and twisted, their stories untold.
I taste their salt on the edge of my tongue,
The bitterness sharp, the words left unsung.

I feel their pull with every step I take,
The weight of their history, a life I forsake.
In the silence, I hear them grow loud,
Roots digging deeper, they shroud and they crowd.

I see their shadows spread wide and tall,
I see them divide me, make me fall.

But in their deep grasp, I must learn to breathe
—And untangle the knots that I can't yet believe.

Echoes from Below

From beneath, the roots still whisper their name,They call me to witness the source of my shame.

I taste their ashes, feel the cold breath,
Of memories buried beneath years of death.

I hear them now, as they gnaw at my soul,
Pulling me under, demanding control.
I feel them burn like a slow, cruel fire,
Their whispers take me higher, then pull me to mire.

The roots of my pain are the soil of my fears,
The seeds of my struggles have bloomed over years.

But what if I stand and face them head-on,
Would I rise from the ashes, or wither and be gone?

CHAPTER TWO

The Weight of Tears

Drowning in the Tide

A river of grief, a flood of despair,
Swallows me whole, consumes every prayer.
The weight of my tears pulls deep like a stone,
In the dark of the night, I feel so alone.

I taste the salt of sorrow on my lips,
Feel the ache of a heart that slowly slips.
I hear the soft sobs that refuse to be still,
As the weight of my tears breaks every will.

Yet in this deep current, a lesson is born,
For only through drowning, we're ever reborn.

Heavy as Heaven

The tears that I shed are heavy as stone,
Weighing me down to the marrow, alone.
I taste the sting of the sorrow I keep,
In the silence of secrets that bury so deep.

Feel the weight on my chest, a crushing force,
Tears like rivers, they run their own course.
The sound of my weeping, a thunderous cry,
As I break and I bend, asking God why.

But heavy as heaven, this grief must be,
For growth lies in weight, in the depth of the
sea.

Shattered Glass

Each tear that falls is a shard of my soul,
Sharp as the edges that make me whole.
I taste the bitterness of broken belief,
A sorrow so deep, it's beyond all relief.

I feel the cold sting of loss on my skin,
Each drop a reminder of where I've been.
I hear the silence that follows the fall,
The weight of my tears, the loudest call.

And yet, as I shatter, I start to rebuild,
For pain is the fire that sharpens the will.

Sinking in Sorrow

I sink in the sea of my sorrow so deep,
A weight on my heart that's too heavy to keep.
I taste the tang of regret on my tongue,
A melody played that is never unsung.

Feel the earth shift beneath me, unkind,
The tears are the anchors that bind and unwind.

I hear the thunder of grief in the air,
It roars in my ears, but I'm unaware.

For in every tear, there's a seed that will grow,
Through the weight of my sorrow, I'll learn how to glow.

The Cry of the Soul

The cry of my soul echoes in the dark,
Tears fall like rain, a permanent mark.
I taste the iron of grief on my breath,
A sharp, bitter tang, a dance with death.

Feel the ache that won't let me be,
The weight of the tears that set my mind free.
I hear the silence scream in my ears,
A symphony played with unspoken fears.

But the cry of my soul will one day be still,
For in sorrow's deep waters, I find my will.

CHAPTER THREE

Breaking the Chains

Shattered Shackles

The chains that clanged in silence and fear,
Now break with a whisper that no one can hear.

Cold iron, once heavy, now falls with a crash,
As I tear through the darkness, no longer abashed.

I taste the rust of the years I was bound,
But now, I feel freedom rising around.
My heart, once shattered, beats loud and strong,

A rhythm of release, where I truly belong.

I hear the chains fall, a symphony of light,
The sound of my soul as it takes flight.

Beneath the Weight

Beneath the weight, I crawled, I cried,
Held by the ghosts that never died.
The walls, once tall, now crumble and fade,
As I step into freedom, unafraid.

I feel the grip loosen, the pull start to cease,
Like burning in water, I find my release.
Taste of bitterness, now turned to sweet,
Each step away is a victory, a beat.

The chains that held me are buried in dust,
For the strength I sought, I now trust.

Unraveling the Past

Each thread that binds, I rip and tear,
Unraveling moments I thought were fair.
The lies that held me are left in the past,
As I break the chains that never could last.

I taste the anger that once left me blind,
Now it's bitterness I leave behind.
I feel the weight of wounds once deep,
But the chains are breaking; I wake from the sleep.

The past is a shadow, but I am the sun,
Rising, releasing, now that I've begun.

The Battle Within

A war rages deep, inside of my skin,
Fighting the darkness that lives within.
But with every tear, I find my might,
As I break through the chains that held me tight.

I feel the cold grip of fear in my veins,
But I rise, undeterred by the pains.
I taste the courage, bitter but bold,
A story of freedom, waiting to unfold.

The chains, now gone, leave a path untold,
A new journey begins, a heart made of gold.

Fractured Chains

The weight of my past, like a heavy cloak,
Crushed every dream, every word I spoke.
But now with each step, the chains start to
crack, And I fight to take my life back.

I taste the dust of broken regret,
But I feel the power of strength unmet.
I hear my voice, once muted with fear,
Now roaring with purpose, crystal clear.

The chains that bound me can never remain,
For I'm free in my soul, untethered from pain.

CHAPTER FOUR

Pruning the Heart

Cutting the Ties

With each cut, a piece of me dies,
The tangled threads, the tangled lies.
I taste the bitterness of love turned cold,
Feel the edges of wounds too sharp to hold.

The weight of the past clings, a heavy vine,
I hear the whispers—"Let go, redefine."
But the silence screams with each breath I take, A heart once whole, now bruised and awake.

I see the scars as they slowly fade,
Leaving behind the strength that was made.

Unraveling the Knots

Knots of doubt in my chest, they twist,
Each one a thought I can't resist.
I feel their pull as they drag me down,
But I know now—it's time to drown.

I taste the ash of all I've believed,
Feel the weight of all I've grieved.
I hear the tug of the old me fight,
But I'll sever the bond, step into the light.

The fibers break with a sharp, clean tear,
And I stand alone, but no longer scared.

The Garden Within

In the soil of my soul, I plant new seeds,
Pulling out roots of old wounds and needs.
I feel the dirt, rough on my skin,
But each tiny wound will heal from within.

I hear the cries of the past as they fade,
Their voices soft, their grip unswayed.
But I taste the sweetness of letting go,
As I prune the thorns where my heart once lay
low.

I see the blooms of a new self rise,
Each petal a truth, unspoken, wise.

The Shredding of Skin

I shed my skin, the weight of the past,

The doubts, the fears, the love that didn't last.

I feel the sting as the layers peel,

But there's freedom in the rawness I feel.

The taste of pain lingers on my tongue,

But the fire inside me is finally sung.

I hear the whispers of strength in the breeze,

As I let go of the chains that used to freeze.

I see myself, reborn and bare,

In the beauty of the wounds I no longer wear.

Cleansing the Soul

I taste the salt of my own regret,
Each tear a cleansing, each loss a debt.
I feel the burn of memories, sharp and bright,
But I stand in the ashes, ready to fight.

I hear the roar of a heart set free,
No longer chained by what used to be.
I see the future, unclouded, clear,
As I prune away the doubt, the fear.

The strength to let go, to heal and grow,
Is found in the shedding, in letting it go.

CHAPTER FIVE

The Storm Within

Thunder in My Soul

The storm rages loud, a deafening roar,
It shakes my spirit, it pounds my core.
I taste the salt of unshed tears,
Feel the weight of unspoken fears.

Thunder cracks in my chest, so wild,
The lightning strikes, my heart defiled.
I hear the cries of my shattered mind,
Yet, in the chaos, I seek what I can't find.

But somewhere beneath the roar, I know—
The storm will pass, and I will grow.

Tornado of Thought

Thoughts whirl like winds, sharp as knives,
Twisting, turning, with fractured lives.
I feel the tug of each memory lost,
Caught in the swirl, no matter the cost.

I taste the smoke of burning dreams,
Feel the force of my shattered seams.
I hear the chaos, it screams and calls,
A hurricane of heartache that never stalls.

But through the cyclone, a light breaks through, In the eye of the storm, I begin anew.

Waves of Worry

Waves crash inside, relentless and strong,
I taste the fear that lingers too long.
I feel the pressure of each rolling tide,
The currents pull me, but I try to hide.

I hear the crashing, it drowns my pleas,
The turmoil echoes like bitter seas.
I see the storm on the edge of my mind,
But somewhere, I know I'll leave it behind.

For the storm within is fierce and real,
But its fury is what I must heal.

The Firestorm Within

Fire burns deep, a raging flame,
Scorched with regrets, I can't untame.
I taste the ash of all I've failed,
Feel the blaze as my soul's assailed.

I hear the crackle of my shattered heart,
The embers flicker, they tear apart.
But through the smoke, I see the glow,
The storm that burns will make me grow.

For in the fire, my strength is born,
And in the storm, my soul is reborn.

The Quiet After

In the aftermath, the air feels thick,
I taste the silence, sharp and quick.
The storm has passed, but left its trace,
A lingering ache I can't erase.

I feel the stillness, broken and new,
The ground beneath me, torn but true.
I hear my breath, slow and deep,
A calm I've earned from chaos I keep.

The storm within has torn me apart,
But in the stillness, I find my heart.

CHAPTER SIX

Finding Faith in the Fall

The Plunge Into Faith

I fell through the dark, my heart a heavy stone,
Lost in the shadows, so far from home.
I taste the bitterness of doubt's cold sting,
But in the fall, I hear faith sing.

Feel the ground slip beneath my feet,
Yet trust in the rise, the promise, the beat.
I see the light in the distance, so small—
And know I'll be caught, after the fall.

For in the plunge, I learn to trust,
That the fall is part of the rise, it's just.

Broken and Whole

Shattered dreams scatter, like glass in the rain,
Yet in each piece, there's healing from pain.
I taste the salt of tears that flow,
But in the flood, my faith starts to grow.

I feel the weight of what I've lost,
The toll of the pain, the deep, cold cost.
But through the cracks, a soft light gleams—
A hope that flows like quiet streams.

I hear the whisper, soft and true,
That faith is born when we're broken in two.

Trust in the Fall

I fall, but the ground is not the end,
Each fall is a lesson, each step a friend.
I taste the earth, gritty and raw,
But I feel the strength to stand in awe.

Through the darkness, I see no way,
But trust the path that leads to the day.
The storm may rage, but in my heart,
I know the rain will cleanse every part.

In the fall, I find my wings,
And in the trust, my spirit sings.

The Struggle and the Rise

I'm lost in the fight, but I'm not alone,

For in the struggle, a strength has grown.

I taste the fire of doubt's harsh kiss,

But feel the spark that pulls me from the abyss.

I hear the thunder of fear, so loud,

But see the light breaking through the cloud.

In each step, I rise and bend,

For trust is the journey that never ends.

The fall is painful, but the rise is divine,

And in the fall, I learn to shine.

Faith Like Water

Like water, I flow, unsure of my course,
Pulled by the tides, a silent force.
I taste the earth as I crash and break,
But feel the healing with every shake.

I hear the roar of the waves inside,
The turbulence where no truths can hide.
Yet in the depths, a calm does grow—
A trust in the flow that I now know.

For faith, like water, will always find its way,
Through every storm, to the light of day.

CHAPTER SEVEN

Repositioning the Soul

The Turning Point

I stand at the crossroads, heart full of doubt,
Tasting the fear that I've lived without.
Feel the weight of the past on my chest,
But the future whispers: "Come, you must rest."

I see the path shift beneath my feet,
The echoes of change, so bitter, so sweet.
I hear the call of a life redefined—
A soul repositioned, a purpose aligned.

In the turning, I know I will find,
A version of me that's no longer confined.

Breaking the Mold

Old ways crumble, like dust in the breeze,
I taste the freedom, and finally, I breathe.
Feel the new world as it opens wide,
The truth within me no longer denied.

The chains I once wore, now fall with a sound,
No longer a prisoner, no longer bound.
I hear my voice rise, firm and clear—
A soul repositioned, no longer in fear.

I see the horizon, so far yet near,
Guiding my steps, as I shift into gear.

A Soul Unfolds

In the quiet, I feel the pull of the light,
A tug in my chest, pulling me from the night.
I taste the sweetness of change on my tongue,
As I step into the life I've just begun.

Feel the weight of the world shift away,
The heavy burden of yesterday's sway.
I hear my heart beat in perfect time,
With the rhythm of growth, so raw, so prime.

I see my reflection—whole, redefined,
A soul reborn, no longer confined.

The Rise of Me

I feel the rise from deep within,
A strength that begins where I have been.
I taste the fire of self anew,
The embers of change that burn so true.

The world may tremble, but I stand tall,
My soul repositioned, answering the call.
I hear the roar of the wind in my ear,
Whispering, "This is your time, never fear."

I see the vision, the purpose, the way,
Leading me forward, each step a new day.

Aligning the Heart

The heart once fractured, now beats as one,
Tasting the sweetness of what's just begun.
Feel the pull of a life realigned,
A soul once lost, now truly defined.

I hear the whispers of truth, soft and clear,
As the old layers fade, I hold them near.
The weight of the past no longer drags,
My heart repositions, no longer in rags.

I see the path where I'm meant to roam,
A soul aligned, finally home.

CHAPTER EIGHT

The Lessons in Every Tear

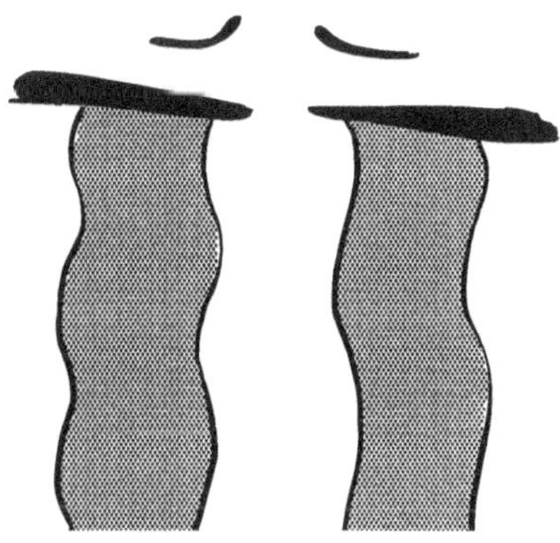

The Wisdom of the Fall

Each tear that falls is a lesson learned,
A fire that scorches, a heart that's burned.
I taste the salt of my own despair,
Yet in each drop, there's wisdom there.

I feel the weight of the pain I've known,
But it's through the hurt that I've grown.
I hear the whispers, soft and clear,
The truth that's found in every tear.

For what is pain but the seed of change?
A lesson wrapped in sorrow's range.

The Echo of Tears

Tears are the echoes of truths unsaid,
The whispers of fears I once had in my head.
I taste the sorrow, but also the strength,
In the depths of my grief, I find my length.

Feel the weight of every broken part,
But I know each fracture shapes my heart.
I hear the lessons, hidden in screams,
Found in the silence between shattered dreams.

For every tear I've shed in vain,
Has taught me to stand, to rise again.

Lessons in the Pain

The pain cuts deep, but there's something more,A lesson hidden behind each sore.
I taste the bitterness of broken trust,
But in this ruin, I learn to adjust.

Feel the tremor of fears that twist,
Yet in their wake, I've found what I missed.
I hear the truth in the quiet cries,
For every tear that falls, I rise.

Each trial, each tear, is a mark of grace,
A lesson found in the darkest place.

The Gift in Grief

Grief is a gift, wrapped in disguise,
I taste the sting of its bitter lies.
Feel the heaviness, a weight so strong,
Yet through the ache, I find where I belong.

I hear the lessons in each sharp sob,
The growth that comes from every job.
For pain is a teacher, rough and real,
But in its lessons, I start to heal.

Every tear I've shed in vain,
Has taught me to stand through the pain.

The Tears that Teach

Each tear that falls is a teacher's word,
A lesson that once seemed unheard.
I taste the salt of my own defeat,
But in the loss, I find what's sweet.

Feel the burden, but see the light,
In the darkest moments, I find my fight.
I hear the lessons in the silence loud,
For tears are the whispers that shape the proud.

Every drop has its own tale to tell,
A story of strength, where once I fell.

CHAPTER NINE

Blossoming Through Adversity

From Ashes to Bloom

From the ashes of pain, I rise,
A flower reborn, reaching for the skies.
I taste the sweetness of battles won,
Feel the warmth of the healing sun.

I see the petals unfurl in grace,
Born from the storm, from the hardest place.
I hear the whispers of strength, soft and clear,
A blossom that bloomed from the weight of
fear.

Through the darkness, I've learned to grow,
And now, I let my beauty show.

The Beauty in Brokenness

Broken, I fell, shattered and torn,
But from the cracks, new life was born.
I taste the bitterness of old regret,
Yet, in my roots, no sorrow is set.

Feel the strength that pushes through,
The wounds now healed, the sky now blue.
I hear the chorus of a soul that sings,
As I spread my wings, shedding old things.

In the brokenness, there's beauty unseen,
A resilience found in what's been torn clean.

Rooted in Struggle

Rooted in struggle, I stand so tall,
Battered by winds, yet I do not fall.
I taste the earth where I've learned to rise,
My strength found in the storm's own cries.

Feel the pull of the earth below,
The weight of the pain that helped me grow.
I hear the wind, it calls me strong,
A song of resilience that's lasted long.

Through the pain, I've found my place,
In adversity's grip, I've learned grace.

Strength in the Storm

The storm raged fierce, it tore my soul,
But from the chaos, I found my whole.
I taste the salt of tears once shed,
Feel the fire that burned, yet led.

I see the lightning, the thunder's roar,
But through it all, I'm so much more.
I hear the call of a heart reborn,
A soul unbroken, no longer torn.

From the tempest, I've learned to rise,
A blossom in the storm, reaching for the skies.

The Rose That Grew

A rose that grew from stone and dust,
In the dark, it bloomed, it learned to trust.
I taste the sweetness of the bloom,
That flourished in the face of doom.

I feel the thorns that once held me tight,
Now they guard the beauty of my light.
I hear the hum of life's soft song,
A melody that's played all along.

Through adversity's grasp, I've found my grace,A rose that flourishes in the hardest place.

CHAPTER TEN

Peace in the Purpose

The Grace of Letting Go

I taste the salt of tears once shed,
But now I see the path ahead.
Feel the weight lift, the burden release,
In the letting go, I find my peace.

The lessons learned, the pain once raw,
Now a gentle whisper, without flaw.
I hear the quiet hum of grace,
As I surrender to the sacred space.

For in the purpose, I find my rest,
Embracing the journey, I'm truly blessed.

Peace in the Flow

I've fought the current, fought the tide,
But now I drift, no longer hide.
Taste the calm of acceptance sweet,
Feel the rhythm of a heart complete.

I see the ripples, soft and wide,
The peace I sought was always inside.
I hear the whispers of fate's sweet call,
That every rise and fall serves us all.

Now I rest, in purpose I trust,
No longer fighting, just flowing...just.

Gratitude for the Wounds

In every wound, there lies a gift,
A scar that helps my spirit lift.
I taste the bitterness, once sharp, once deep,
But now it's the sweetness I choose to keep.

Feel the peace as the edges fade,
In every bruise, a lesson laid.
I hear the hum of a soul reborn,
In gratitude, my heart is worn.

For all the trials have shaped my face,
And now I rest in their embrace.

The Peace of Knowing

I've walked the road, both dark and long,

But now I sing a different song.

Taste the sweetness of my tears,

For they've washed away my deepest fears.

Feel the stillness in my chest,

A knowing that this life is blessed.

I see the purpose in every fall,

And hear the peace that answers the call.

In acceptance, my soul is free,

At last, I've found the peace in me.

The Final Breath

I stand at the end, yet it feels like a start,
Gratitude blooming deep in my heart.
Taste the stillness, a calm I've earned,
Feel the peace, for which I've yearned.

I hear the echo of lessons learned,
The light of purpose, brightly burned.
See the beauty in every scar,
For I know now just how far.

With peace in my soul, I breathe and sigh,
For the purpose was always mine to find.

Final Note

Thank You

Dear Reader,

Thank you for taking the time to journey through Shaped by Tears. Your presence here means the world to me. I hope these words resonated with you, offering comfort, reflection, or simply a moment of connection.

If you enjoyed this collection, I kindly ask you to leave an honest review—it helps others discover these poems and supports my creative work.

Feel free to explore my other poems as well; I'd love for you to experience more of the stories I've shaped through words.

With gratitude,
Taylor Quill

About the Author

Taylor Quill is a contemporary poet and writer known for her evocative and heartfelt explorations of love, resilience, and personal growth. Born and raised in the Pacific Northwest, Taylor draws inspiration from the natural world and the complexities of human experience.

With a background in creative writing and psychology, Taylor's work is infused with empathy, vulnerability, and a deep understanding of the human condition. Her poetry invites readers to reflect on their own journeys, embracing the beauty and complexity of life.

Other Books From Taylor Quill